Wish Upon a Star

igloobooks

Every night, at bedtime, Baby Bear and his mummy loved to snuggle up close on his warm, cosy bed and read a story.

When the story ended, Mummy would tuck Baby Bear up tight,
give him a big cuddle and turn out the light.

One night, when the room went dark, Baby Bear began to feel frightened. "Please leave the light on," he called.

"I'm scared of the dark!"

"Don't be afraid," said Mummy, taking Baby Bear's hand and leading him to the window. "Not everything about night-time is dark. Look outside and see how magical it can be."

Through the window,
Baby Bear could see
that the sky was filled
with bright, shining stars.
"Why don't you make a
wish?" said Mummy.
"I wish I wasn't so afraid
of the dark," whispered
Baby Bear.

As he spoke, one little
star began to shimmer
and shake. Then, suddenly,
it shot across the sky in
a shower of sparkles.
The bears watched in
amazement as it flew past
the window and landed
in their garden.

"Quick!" called Mummy, racing downstairs to see the star.

"Wait for me!" cried Baby Bear, grabbing his teddy and following behind.

"Look," whispered Mummy, opening the door.
Baby Bear gasped. He could see the star glowing in the darkness.
"Let's go and see if we can find it," said Mummy.

Mummy stepped outside and Baby Bear peeked out from behind her.
The garden seemed huge and dark and scary.

Something flew over their heads and hooted with a loud, "Twit-twoo!"
"I don't like it," said Baby Bear. "I don't want to go out there!"

"Come on. Let's be brave together," said Mummy, squeezing Baby Bear's hand. "It will be an adventure."

Baby Bear nodded and gave Teddy a squeeze
to make sure he wasn't scared either.

They hadn't gone far, when Baby Bear saw some lights twinkling in the leaves around him. "Are those shooting stars, too?" he asked.

"Those are fireflies," replied Mummy. "They light up at night."
"Wow!" said Baby Bear. "They're not scary at all.
Are there other animals that come out at night?"

"Yes, look over there," said Mummy, pointing.
"Those bunnies are playing together in the moonlight."
"That looks like fun," said Baby Bear, giggling.

Further along the path, Baby Bear heard the
hooting sound that had frightened him before. "Twit-twoo!"
"What's that?" he cried, hiding behind Mummy.

"It's just an owl," said Mummy, smiling.

"Hello, Owl," said Baby Bear. "We're looking for a fallen star.
Have you seen it?" The owl hooted again and Baby Bear laughed.

Baby Bear could see that the shimmery light of the star
wasn't far away. He was so excited he couldn't wait to see it.
"Come on, Mummy," he said. "We're almost there!"

The bears hurried ahead until they finally spotted
the star lying in the grass. It glittered and glowed brightly.
Little bunnies hopped around it, wondering what it was.

Baby Bear picked up the star and smiled. "It's so bright," he whispered. "I'm going to take it home to light up my room."

Baby Bear and Mummy held on to the star together
and headed back to the house, past the hooting owl,
the hopping bunnies and the flickering fireflies.

Back in bed, Baby Bear tucked the star under his pillow to keep it safe. "Goodnight, Baby Bear," said Mummy. "Goodnight, Mummy," replied Baby Bear.

This time, when Mummy turned out the light,
Baby Bear wasn't scared at all. His special star sparkled
in the darkness, as he snuggled up sleepily.

Baby Bear fell asleep, dreaming of all the wonderful
things he had seen on his adventure. After that night,
he was never afraid of the dark again.